Snow White
and Other Fairy Tales

JACOB AND WILHELM GRIMM

Illustrated by Thea Kliros

DOVER PUBLICATIONS, INC.
New York

DOVER CHILDREN'S THRIFT CLASSICS

EDITOR OF THIS VOLUME: CANDACE WARD

Copyright

Published in Canada by General Publishing Company, Ltd., 30 Lesmill Road, Don Mills, Toronto, Ontario.

Published in the United Kingdom by Constable and Company, Ltd., 3 The Lanchesters, 162–164 Fulham Palace Road, London W6 9ER.

Bibliographical Note

Snow White and Other Fairy Tales, first published by Dover Publications, Inc., in 1994, is a new collection containing the unabridged text of eleven tales from the following: *Household Stories, from the Collection of the Bros. Grimm,* translated by Lucy Crane, originally published by Macmillan and Company, New York, in 1886 ("Snow White," "The Queen Bee," "The Fisherman and His Wife," "The Brave Little Tailor," "The Elves and the Shoemaker," "The Goose Girl"); *Grimm's Fairy Tales,* originally published by T. and A. Constable, Edinburgh, n.d. [1909] ("Doctor Know-all," "The Seven Ravens," "The Lady and the Lion," "Jorinda and Joringel," "The Twelve Dancing Princesses").

Library of Congress Cataloging-in-Publication Data

Kinder- und Hausmärchen. English. Selections
    Snow White and other fairy tales / Jacob and Wilhelm Grimm ; illustrated by Thea Kliros.
        p.   cm. — (Dover children's thrift classics)
    Contents: Snow White — The queen bee — The fisherman and his wife — The brave little tailor — Doctor Know-all — The seven ravens — The elves and the shoemaker — The lady and the lion — The goose girl — Jorinda and Joringel — The twelve dancing princesses.
   ISBN 0-486-28327-5 (pbk.)
    1. Fairy tales—Germany. [1. Fairy tales. 2. Folklore—Germany.] I. Grimm, Jacob, 1785–1863. II. Grimm, Wilhelm, 1786–1859. III. Kliros, Thea, ill. IV. Title. V. Series.
PZ8.K57   1994
398.2′0943—dc20   94-32381
                                                CIP
                                              AC

Manufactured in the United States of America
Dover Publications, Inc., 31 East 2nd Street, Mineola, N.Y. 11501

Note

In 1806, the Brothers Grimm, Jacob Ludwig Carl (1785–1863) and Wilhelm Carl (1786–1859), began collecting popular tales of their native Germany. While such collections were not unusual in the nineteenth century, the Grimms' two-volume *Kinder- und Hausmärchen* ("Nursery and Household Tales"), containing over 200 tales, was immensely popular and influential. The brothers' initial purpose was to gather the tales while oral storytellers were still practicing their craft. They strongly believed that the oral tradition was an important part of Germany's literary heritage, and that the only way to preserve the tales was to record them just as they were told. One of their sources was a tailor's wife, Katharina Viehmann, who provided the brothers with twenty tales, including "The Goose Girl," included here; another source was an old soldier, who told his tales in return for gifts of old trousers.

From the first, the Grimms' collection was an immediate success with children, despite the inclusion of scholarly apparatus and notes in the early editions and an absence of illustrations. In all, the tales from *Kinder- und Hausmärchen* were translated into 70 languages, and subsequent editions and translations were designed especially for children. The eleven fairy tales presented here are among the best-loved and are sure to delight children of all ages, whether they are reading them for the first or the hundredth time.

Contents

List of Illustrations

Snow White

IT WAS the middle of winter, and the snow-flakes were falling like feathers from the sky, and a queen sat at her window working, and her embroidery frame was of ebony. And as she worked, gazing at times out on the snow, she pricked her finger, and there fell from it three drops of blood on the snow. And when she saw how bright and red it looked, she said to herself, "Oh that I had a child as white as snow, as red as blood, and as black as the wood of the embroidery frame!"

Not very long after she had a daughter, with a skin as white as snow, lips as red as blood, and hair as black as ebony, and she was named Snow White. And when she was born the queen died.

After a year had gone by the king took another wife, a beautiful woman, but proud and over-bearing, and she could not bear to be surpassed in beauty by any one. She had a magic looking glass, and she used to stand before it, and look in it, and say,

1

> "Looking glass upon the wall,
> Who is fairest of us all?"

And the looking glass would answer,

> "You are fairest of them all."

And she was contented, for she knew that the looking glass spoke the truth.

Now, Snow White was growing prettier and prettier, and when she was seven years old she was as beautiful as day, far more so than the queen herself. So one day when the queen went to her mirror and said,

> "Looking glass upon the wall,
> Who is fairest of us all?"

It answered,

> "Queen, you are full fair, 'tis true,
> But Snow White fairer is than you."

This gave the queen a great shock, and she became yellow and green with envy, and from that hour her heart turned against Snow White, and she hated her. And envy and pride like ill weeds grew in her heart higher every day, until she had no peace day or night. At last she sent for a huntsman, and said,

"Take the child out into the woods, so that I may set eyes on her no more. You must put her to death, and bring me her heart for a token."

The huntsman consented, and led her away; but when he drew his cutlass to pierce Snow White's innocent heart, she began to weep, and to say,

"Oh, dear huntsman, do not take my life; I will go away into the wild wood, and never come home again."

And as she was so lovely the huntsman had pity on her, and said,

"Away with you then, poor child"; for he thought the wild animals would be sure to devour her, and it was as if a stone had been rolled away from his heart when he spared to put her to death. Just at that moment a young wild boar came running by, so he caught and killed it, and taking out its heart, he brought it to the queen for a token. And it was salted and cooked, and the wicked woman ate it up, thinking that there was as end of Snow White.

Now, when the poor child found herself quite alone in the wild woods, she felt full of terror, even of the very leaves on the trees, and she did not know what to do for fright. Then she began to run over the sharp stones and through the thorn bushes, and the wild beasts after her, but they did her no harm. She ran as long as her feet would carry her; and when the evening drew near she came to a little house, and she went inside to rest. Everything there was very small, but as pretty and clean as possible. There stood the little table ready laid, and covered with a white cloth, and seven little plates, and seven knives and forks, and drinking cups. By the wall stood seven little beds, side by side, covered with clean white quilts. Snow White, being very hungry and thirsty, ate from each plate a little porridge and bread, and drank out of each little cup a drop of wine, so as not to finish up one portion alone. After that she felt so tired that she lay down on one of the beds, but it did not seem to suit her; one was too long, another too short, but at last the seventh was quite right; and so she lay down upon it, committed herself to heaven, and fell asleep.

When it was quite dark, the masters of the house came home. They were seven dwarfs, whose occupation was to dig underground among the mountains. When they had lighted their seven candles, and it was quite light in the little house, they saw that some one must have been in, as everything was not in the same order in which they left it. The first said,

"Who has been sitting in my little chair?"

The second said,

"Who has been eating from my little plate?"

The third said,

"Who has been taking my little loaf?"

The fourth said,

"Who has been tasting my porridge?"

The fifth said,

"Who has been using my little fork?"

The sixth said,

"Who has been cutting with my little knife?"

The seventh said,

"Who has been drinking from my little cup?"

Then the first one, looking round, saw a hollow in his bed, and cried,

"Who has been lying on my bed?"

And the others came running, and cried,

"Some one has been on our beds too!"

But when the seventh looked at his bed, he saw little Snow White lying there asleep. Then he told the others, who came running up, crying out in their astonishment, and holding up their seven little candles to throw a light upon Snow White.

"O goodness! O gracious!" cried they, "what beautiful child is this?" and were so full of joy to see her that they did not wake her, but let her sleep on. And the seventh dwarf slept with his comrades, an hour at a time with each, until the night had passed.

When it was morning, and Snow White awoke and saw the seven dwarfs, she was very frightened; but they seemed quite friendly, and asked her what her name was, and she told them; and then they asked how she came to be in their house. And she related to them how her stepmother had wished her to be put to death, and how the huntsman had spared her life, and how she had run the whole day long, until at last she had found their little house. Then the dwarfs said,

"If you will keep our house for us, and cook, and wash, and make the beds, and sew and knit, and keep everything tidy and clean, you may stay with us, and you shall lack nothing."

"With all my heart," said Snow White; and so she stayed, and kept the house in good order. In the morning the dwarfs went to the mountain to dig for gold; in the evening they came home, and their supper had to be ready for them. All the day long the maiden was left alone, and the good little dwarfs warned her, saying,

"Beware of your stepmother, she will soon know you are here. Let no one into the house."

Now the queen, having eaten Snow White's heart, as she supposed, felt quite sure that now she was the first and fairest, and so she came to her mirror, and said,

> "Looking glass upon the wall,
>   Who is fairest of us all?"

And the glass answered,

> "Queen, thou art of beauty rare,
>   But Snow White living in the glen
>   With the seven little men
>   Is a thousand times more fair."

Then she was very angry, for the glass always spoke the truth, and she knew that the huntsman must have deceived her, and that Snow White must still be living. And she thought and thought how she could manage to make an end of her, for as long as she was not the fairest in the land,

"Queen, thou art of beauty rare, / But Snow White
living in the glen / With the seven little men / Is a
thousand times more fair."

envy left her no rest. At last she thought of a plan; she painted her face and dressed herself like an old pedlar woman, so that no one would have known her. In this disguise she went across the seven mountains, until she came to the house of the seven little dwarfs, and she knocked at the door and cried,

"Fine wares to sell! fine wares to sell!"

Snow White peeped out of the window and cried,

"Good-day, good woman, what have you to sell?"

"Good wares, fine wares," answered she, "laces of all colours"; and she held up a piece that was woven of variegated silk.

"I need not be afraid of letting in this good woman," thought Snow White, and she unbarred the door and bought the pretty lace.

"What a figure you are, child!" said the old woman, "come and let me lace you properly for once."

Snow White, suspecting nothing, stood up before her, and let her lace her with the new lace; but the old woman laced so quick and tight that it took Snow White's breath away, and she fell down as dead.

"Now you have done with being the fairest," said the old woman as she hastened away.

Not long after that, towards evening, the seven dwarfs came home, and were terrified to see their dear Snow White lying on the ground, without life or motion; they raised her up, and when they saw how tightly she was laced they cut the lace in two; then she began to draw breath, and little by little she returned to life. When the dwarfs heard what had happened they said,

"The old pedlar woman was no other than the wicked queen; you must beware of letting any one in when we are not here!"

And when the wicked woman got home she went to her glass and said,

> "Looking glass against the wall,
>   Who is fairest of us all?"

And it answered as before,

> "Queen, thou art of beauty rare,
>   But Snow White living in the glen
>   With the seven little men
>   Is a thousand times more fair."

When she heard that she was so struck with surprise that all the blood left her heart, for she knew that Snow White must still be living.

"But now," said she, "I will think of something that will be her ruin." And by witchcraft she made a poisoned comb. Then she dressed herself up to look like another different sort of old woman. So she went across the seven mountains and came to the house of the seven dwarfs, and knocked at the door and cried,

"Good wares to sell! good wares to sell!"

Snow White looked out and said,

"Go away, I must not let anybody in."

"But you are not forbidden to look," said the old woman, taking out the poisoned comb and holding it up. It pleased the poor child so much that she was tempted to open the door; and when the bargain was made the old woman said,

"Now, for once your hair shall be properly combed."

Poor Snow White, thinking no harm, let the old woman do as she would, but no sooner was the comb put in her hair than the poison began to work, and the poor girl fell down senseless.

"Now, you paragon of beauty," said the wicked woman, "this is the end of you," and went off. By good luck it was now near evening, and the seven little dwarfs came home. When they saw Snow White lying on the ground as dead, they thought directly that it was the stepmother's doing, and looked about, found the poisoned comb, and no sooner had they drawn it out of her hair than Snow White came to herself, and related all that had passed. Then they warned her once more to be on her guard, and never again to let any one in at the door.

And the queen went home and stood before the looking glass and said,

"Looking glass against the wall,
Who is fairest of us all?"

And the looking glass answered as before,

> "Queen, thou art of beauty rare,
> But Snow White living in the glen
> With the seven little men
> Is a thousand times more fair."

When she heard the looking glass speak thus she trembled and shook with anger.

"Snow White shall die," cried she, "though it should cost me my own life!" And then she went to a secret lonely chamber, where no one was likely to come, and there she made a poisonous apple. It was beautiful to look upon, being white with red cheeks, so that any one who should see it must long for it, but whoever ate even a little bit of it must die. When the apple was ready she painted her face and clothed herself like a peasant woman, and went across the seven mountains to where the seven dwarfs lifed. And when she knocked at the door Snow White put her head out of the window and said,

"I dare not let anybody in; the seven dwarfs told me not."

"All right," answered the woman; "I can easily get rid of my apples elsewhere. There, I will give you one."

"No," answered Snow White, "I dare not take anything."

"Are you afraid of poison?" said the woman, "look here, I will cut the apple in two pieces; you shall have the red side, I will have the white one."

For the apple was so cunningly made, that all the poison was in the rosy half of it. Snow White longed for the beautiful apple, and as she saw the peasant woman eating a piece of it she could no longer refrain, but stretched out her hand and took the poisoned half. But no sooner had she taken a morsel of it into her mouth than she fell to the earth as dead. And the queen, casting on her a terrible glance, laughed aloud and cried,

"As white as snow, as red as blood, as black as ebony! this time the dwarfs will not be able to bring you to life again."

And when she went home and asked the looking glass,

> "Looking glass against the wall,
> Who is fairest of us all?"

at last it answered,

"You are the fairest now of all."

Then her envious heart had peace, as much as an envious heart can have.

The dwarfs, when they came home in the evening, found Snow White lying on the ground, and there came no breath out of her mouth, and she was dead. They lifted her up, sought if anything poisonous was to be found, cut her laces, combed her hair, washed her with water and wine, but all was of no avail, the poor child was dead, and remained dead. Then they laid her on a bier, and sat all seven of them round it, and wept and lamented three whole days. And then they would have buried her, but that she looked still as if she were living, with her beautiful blooming cheeks. So they said,

"We cannot hide her away in the black ground." And they had made a coffin of clear glass, so as to be looked into from all sides, and they laid her in it, and wrote in golden letters upon it her name, and that she was a king's daughter. Then they set the coffin out upon the mountain, and one of them always remained by it to watch. And the birds came too, and mourned for Snow White, first an owl, then a raven, and lastly, a dove.

Now, for a long while Snow White lay in the coffin and never changed, but looked as if she were asleep, for she was still as white as snow, as red as blood, and her hair was as black as ebony. It happened, however, that one day a king's son rode through the wood and up to the dwarfs' house, which was near it. He saw on the mountain the coffin, and beautiful Snow White within it, and he read what was written in golden letters upon it. Then he said to the dwarfs,

"Let me have the coffin, and I will give you whatever you like to ask for it."

But the dwarfs told him that they could not part with it for all the gold in the world. But he said,

"I beseech you to give it me, for I cannot live

without looking upon Snow White; if you consent I will bring you to great honour, and care for you as if you were my brethren."

When he so spoke the good little dwarfs had pity upon him and gave him the coffin, and the king's son called his servants and bid them carry it away on their shoulders. Now it happened that as they were going along they stumbled over a bush, and with the shaking the bit of poisoned apple flew out of her throat. It was not long before she opened her eyes, threw up the cover of the coffin, and sat up, alive and well.

"Oh dear! where am I?" cried she. The king's son answered, full of joy, "You are near me," and, relating all that had happened, he said,

"I would rather have you than anything in the world; come with me to my father's castle and you shall be my bride."

And Snow White was kind, and went with him, and their wedding was held with pomp and great splendour.

But Snow White's wicked stepmother was also bidden to the feast, and when she had dressed herself in beautiful clothes she went to her looking glass and said,

> "Looking glass upon the wall,
> Who is fairest of us all?"

The looking glass answered,

"O Queen, although you are of beauty rare,
  The young bride is a thousand times more fair."

Then she railed and cursed, and was beside
herself with disappointment and anger. First she
thought she would not go to the wedding; but
then she felt she should have no peace until she
went and saw the bride. And when she saw her
she knew her for Snow White, and could not stir
from the place for anger and terror. For they had
ready red-hot iron shoes, in which she had to
dance until she fell down dead.

The Queen Bee

TWO KING'S sons once started to seek adventures, and fell into a wild, reckless way of living, and gave up all thoughts of going home again. Their third and youngest brother, who was called Witling, and had remained behind, started off to seek them; and when at last he found them, they jeered at his simplicity in thinking that he could make his way in the world, while they who were so much cleverer were unsuccessful. But they all three went on together until they came to an ant hill, which the two eldest brothers wished to stir up, that they might see the little ants hurry about in their fright and carrying off their eggs, but Witling said,

"Leave the little creatures alone, I will not suffer them to be disturbed."

And they went on farther until they came to a lake, where a number of ducks were swimming about. The two eldest brothers wanted to catch a couple and cook them, but Witling would not allow it, and said, "Leave the creatures alone, I will not suffer them to be killed."

16

And then they came to a bee's nest in a tree, and there was so much honey in it that it overflowed and ran down the trunk. The two eldest brothers then wanted to make a fire beneath the tree, that the bees might be stifled by the smoke, and then they could get at the honey. But Witling prevented them, saying,

"Leave the little creatures alone, I will not suffer them to be stifled."

At last the three brothers came to a castle where there were in the stables many horses standing, all of stone, and the brothers went through all the rooms until they came to a door at the end secured with three locks, and in the middle of the door a small opening through which they could look into the room. And they saw a little grey-haired man sitting at a table. They called out to him once, twice, and he did not hear, but at the third time he got up, undid the locks, and came out. Without speaking a word he led them to a table loaded with all sorts of good things, and when they had eaten and drunk he showed to each his bedchamber. The next morning the little grey man came to the eldest brother, and beckoning him, brought him to a table of stone, on which were written three things directing by what means the castle could be delivered from its enchantment. The first thing was, that in the wood under the moss lay the pearls belonging to the princess—a thousand in number—and they were to be sought for and collected, and if he who should undertake the task had not finished it by sunset,—if but one pearl were missing,—he must be turned to stone. So the eldest brother went out, and searched all day, but at the end of it he had only found one hundred; just as was said on the table of stone came to pass and he was turned into stone. The second brother undertook the adventure next day, but it fared with him no better than with the first; he found two hundred pearls, and was turned into stone.

And so at last it was Witling's turn, and he began to search in the moss; but it was a very tedious business to find the pearls, and he grew so out of heart that he sat down on a stone and began to weep. As he was sitting thus, up came the ant king with five thousand ants, whose lives had been saved through Witling's pity, and it was not very long before the little insects had collected all the pearls and put them in a heap.

Now the second thing ordered by the table of stone was to get the key of the princess's sleeping chamber out of the lake.

And when Witling came to the lake, the ducks whose lives he had saved came swimming, and dived below, and brought up the key from the bottom. The third thing that had to be done was the most difficult, and that was to choose out the youngest and loveliest of the three princesses, as they lay sleeping. All bore a perfect resemblance each to the other, and only differed in this, that before they went to sleep each one had eaten a different sweetmeat,—the eldest a piece of sugar, the second a little syrup, and the third a spoonful of honey. Now the Queen bee of those bees that Witling had protected from the fire came at this moment, and trying the lips of all three, settled on those of the one that had eaten honey, and so it was that the king's son knew which to choose. Then the spell was broken; every one awoke from stony sleep, and took their right form again.

And Witling married the youngest and loveliest princess, and became king after her father's death. But his two brothers had to put up with the two other sisters.

The Fisherman and His Wife

THERE WAS once a fisherman and his wife who lived together in a hovel by the sea-shore, and the fisherman went out every day with his hook and line to catch fish, and he angled and angled.

One day he was sitting with his rod and looking into the clear water, and he sat and sat.

At last down went the line to the bottom of the water, and when he drew it up he found a great flounder on the hook. And the flounder said to him,

"Fisherman, listen to me; let me go, I am not a real fish but an enchanted prince. What good shall I be to you if you land me? I shall not taste well; so put me back into the water again, and let me swim away."

"Well," said the fisherman, "no need of so many words about the matter, as you can speak I had much rather let you swim away."

Then he put him back into the clear water, and the flounder sank to the bottom, leaving a long streak of blood behind him. Then the fisherman got up and went home to his wife in their hovel.

"Well, husband," said the wife, "have you caught nothing today?"

"No," said the man—"that is, I did catch a flounder, but as he said he was an enchanted prince, I let him go again."

"Then, did you wish for nothing?" said the wife.

"No," said the man; "what should I wish for?"

"Oh dear!" said the wife; "and it is so dreadful always to live in this evil-smelling hovel; you might as well have wished for a little cottage; go again and call him; tell him we want a little cottage, I daresay he will give it us; go, and be quick."

And when he went back, the sea was green and yellow, and not nearly so clear. So he stood and said,

> "O man, O man!—if man you be,
> Or flounder, flounder, in the sea—
> Such a tiresome wife I've got,
> For she wants what I do not."

Then the flounder came swimming up, and said,

"Now then, what does she want?"

"Oh," said the man, "you know when I caught you my wife says I ought to have wished for something. She does not want to live any longer in the hovel, and would rather have a cottage."

"Go home with you," said the flounder, "she has it already."

So the man went home, and found, instead of the hovel, a little cottage, and his wife was sitting on a bench before the door. And she took him by the hand, and said to him,

"Come in and see if this is not a great improvement."

So they went in, and there was a little house-place and a beautiful little bedroom, a kitchen and larder, with all sorts of furniture, and iron and brass ware of the very best. And at the back was a little yard with fowls and ducks, and a little garden full of green vegetables and fruit.

"Look," said the wife, "is not that nice?"

"Yes," said the man, "if this can only last we shall be very well contented."

"We will see about that," said the wife. And after a meal they went to bed.

So all went well for a week or fortnight, when the wife said,

"Look here, husband, the cottage is really too confined, and the yard and garden are so small; I think the flounder had better get us a larger house; I should like very much to live in a large stone castle; so go to your fish and he will send us a castle."

"O my dear wife," said the man, "the cottage is good enough; what do we want a castle for?"

"We want one," said the wife; "go along with you; the flounder can give us one."

"Now, wife," said the man, "the flounder gave us the cottage; I do not like to go to him again, he may be angry."

"Go along," said the wife, "he might just as well give us it as not; do as I say!"

The man felt very reluctant and unwilling; and he said to himself,

"It is not the right thing to do;" nevertheless he went.

So when he came to the seaside, the water was purple and dark blue and grey and thick, and not green and yellow as before. And he stood and said,

> "O man, O man!—if man you be,
> Or flounder, flounder, in the sea—
> Such a tiresome wife I've got,
> For she wants what I do not."

"Now then, what does she want?" said the flounder.

"Oh," said the man, half frightened, "she wants to live in a large stone castle."

"Go home with you, she is already standing before the door," said the flounder.

Then the man went home, as he supposed, but when he got there, there stood in the place of the cottage a great castle of stone, and his wife was standing on the steps, about to go in; so she took him by the hand, and said,

"Let us enter."

With that he went in with her, and in the castle was a great hall with a marble pavement, and there were a great many servants, who led them through large doors, and the passages were decked with tapestry, and the rooms with golden chairs and tables, and crystal chandeliers hanging from the ceiling; and all the rooms had carpets. And the tables were covered with eatables and the best wine for any one who wanted them. And at the back of the house was a great stableyard for horses and cattle, and carriages of the finest; besides, there was a splendid large garden, with the most beautiful flowers and fine fruit trees, and a pleasance full half a mile long, with deer and oxen and sheep, and everything that heart could wish for.

"There!" said the wife, "is not this beautiful?"

"Oh yes," said the man, "if it will only last we can live in this fine castle and be very well contented."

"We will see about that," said the wife, "in the meanwhile we will sleep upon it." With that they went to bed.

The next morning the wife was awake first, just at the break of day, and she looked out and saw from her bed the beautiful country lying all round. The man took no notice of it, so she poked him in the side with her elbow, and said,

"Husband, get up and just look out of the window. Look, just think if we could be king over all this country. Just go to your fish and tell him we should like to be king."

"Now, wife," said the man, "what should we be kings for? I don't want to be king."

"Well," said the wife, "if you don't want to be king, I will be king."

"Now, wife," said the man, "what do you want

to be king for? I could not ask him such a thing."

"Why not?" said the wife, "you must go directly all the same; I must be king."

So the man went, very much put out that his wife should want to be king.

"It is not the right thing to do—not at all the right thing," thought the man. He did not at all want to go, and yet he went all the same.

And when he came to the sea the water was quite dark grey, and rushed far inland, and had an ill smell. And he stood and said,

> "O man, O man!—if man you be,
> Or flounder, flounder, in the sea—
> Such a tiresome wife I've got,
> For she wants what I do not."

"Now then, what does she want?" said the fish.

"Oh dear!" said the man, "she wants to be king."

"Go home with you, she is so already," said the fish.

So the man went back, and as he came to the palace he saw it was very much larger, and had great towers and splendid gateways; the herald stood before the door, and a number of soldiers with kettle-drums and trumpets.

And when he came inside everything was of marble and gold, and there were many curtains with great golden tassels. Then he went through the doors of the saloon to where the great throne-room was, and there was his wife sitting upon a throne of gold and diamonds, and she had a great golden crown on, and the sceptre in her hand was of pure gold and jewels, and on each side stood six pages in a row, each one a head shorter than the other. So the man went up to her and said,

"Well, wife, so now you are king!"

"Yes," said the wife, "now I am king."

So then he stood and looked at her, and when he had gazed at her for some time he said,

"Well, wife, this is fine for you to be king! now there is nothing more to wish for."

"O husband!" said the wife, seeming quite restless, "I am tired of this already. Go to your fish and tell him that now I am king I must be emperor."

"Now, wife," said the man, "what do you want to be emperor for?"

"Husband," said she, "go and tell the fish I want to be emperor."

"Oh dear!" said the man, "he could not do it— I cannot ask him such a thing. There is but one emperor at a time; the fish can't possibly make any one emperor—indeed he can't."

"Now, look here," said the wife, "I am king, and you are only my husband, so will you go at once? Go along! for if he was able to make me king he is able to make me emperor; and I will and must be emperor, so go along!"

So he was obliged to go; and as he went he

felt very uncomfortable about it, and he thought to himself,

"It is not at all the right thing to do; to want to be emperor is really going too far; the flounder will soon be beginning to get tired of this."

With that he came to the sea, and the water was quite black and thick, and the foam flew, and the wind blew, and the man was terrified. But he stood and said,

> "O man, O man!—if man you be,
>   Or flounder, flounder, in the sea—
>   Such a tiresome wife I've got,
>   For she wants what I do not."

"What is it now?" said the fish.

"Oh dear!" said the man, "my wife wants to be emperor."

"Go home with you," said the fish, "she is emperor already."

So the man went home, and found the castle adorned with polished marble and alabaster figures, and golden gates. The troops were being marshalled before the door, and they were blowing trumpets and beating drums and cymbals; and when he entered he saw barons and earls and dukes waiting about like servants; and the doors were of bright gold. And he saw his wife sitting upon a throne made of one entire piece of gold, and it was about two miles high; and she had a great golden crown on, which was about

With that he came to the sea, and the water was quite black and thick, and the foam flew, and the wind blew, and the man was terrified.

three yards high, set with brilliants and car-
buncles; and in one hand she held the sceptre,
and in the other the globe; and on both sides of
her stood pages in two rows, all arranged accord-
ing to their size, from the most enormous giant
of two miles high to the tiniest dwarf of the size
of my little finger; and before her stood earls and
dukes in crowds. So the man went up to her and
said,

"Well, wife, so now you are emperor."

"Yes," said she, "now I am emperor."

Then he went and sat down and had a good
look at her, and then he said,

"Well now, wife, there is nothing left to be,
now you are emperor."

"What are you talking about, husband?" said
she; "I am emperor, and next I will be pope! so
go and tell the fish so."

"Oh dear!" said the man, "what is it that you
don't want? You can never become pope; there is
but one pope in Christendom, and the fish can't
possibly do it."

"Husband," said she, "no more words about it;
I must and will be pope; so go along to the fish."

"Now, wife," said the man, "how can I ask him
such a thing? it is too bad—it is asking a little
too much; and, besides, he could not do it."

"What rubbish!" said the wife; "if he could
make me emperor he can make me pope. Go
along and ask him; I am emperor, and you are
only my husband, so go you must."

So he went, feeling very frightened, and he shivered and shook, and his knees trembled; and there arose a great wind, and the clouds flew by, and it grew very dark, and the sea rose mountains high, and the ships were tossed about, and the sky was partly blue in the middle, but at the sides very dark and red, as in a great tempest. And he felt very desponding, and stood trembling and said,

> "O man, O man!—if man you be,
> Or flounder, flounder, in the sea—
> Such a tiresome wife I've got,
> For she wants what I do not."

"Well, what now?" said the fish.

"Oh dear!" said the man, "she wants to be pope."

"Go home with you, she is pope already," said the fish.

So he went home, and he found himself before a great church, with palaces all round. He had to make his way through a crowd of people; and when he got inside he found the place lighted up with thousands and thousands of lights; and his wife was clothed in a golden garment, and sat upon a very high throne, and had three golden crowns on, all in the greatest priestly pomp; and on both sides of her there stood two rows of lights of all sizes—from the size of the longest tower to the smallest rushlight, and all the emperors and kings were kneeling before her and kissing her foot.

"Well, wife," said the man, and sat and stared at her, "so you are pope."

"Yes," said she, "now I am pope!"

And he went on gazing at her till he felt dazzled, as if he were sitting in the sun. And after a little time he said,

"Well, now, wife, what is there left to be, now you are pope?"

And she sat up very stiff and straight, and said nothing.

And he said again, "Well, wife, I hope you are contented at last with being pope; you can be nothing more."

"We will see about that," said the wife. With that they both went to bed; but she was as far as ever from being contented, and she could not get to sleep for thinking of what she should like to be next.

The husband, however, slept as fast as a top after his busy day; but the wife tossed and turned from side to side the whole night through, thinking all the while what she could be next, but nothing would occur to her; and when she saw the red dawn she slipped off the bed, and sat before the window to see the sun rise, and as it came up she said,

"Ah, I have it! what if I should make the sun and moon to rise—husband!" she cried, and stuck her elbow in his ribs, "wake up, and go to your fish, and tell him I want power over the sun and moon."

The man was so fast asleep that when he started up he fell out of bed. Then he shook himself together, and opened his eyes and said,

"Oh,—wife, what did you say?"

"Husband," said she, "if I cannot get the power of making the sun and moon rise when I want them, I shall never have another quiet hour. Go to the fish and tell him so."

"O wife!" said the man, and fell on his knees to her, "the fish can really not do that for you. I grant you he could make you emperor and pope; do be contented with that, I beg of you."

And she became wild with impatience, and screamed out,

"I can wait no longer, go at once!"

And so off he went as well as he could for fright. And a dreadful storm arose, so that he could hardly keep his feet; and the houses and trees were blown down, and the mountains trembled, and rocks fell in the sea; the sky was quite black, and it thundered and lightened; and the waves, crowned with foam, ran mountains high. So he cried out, without being able to hear his own words,

> "O man, O man!—if man you be,
>   Or flounder, flounder, in the sea—
>   Such a tiresome wife I've got,
>   For she wants what I do not."

"Well, what now?" said the flounder.

"Oh dear!" said the man, "she wants to order about the sun and moon."

"Go home with you!" said the flounder, "you will find her in the old hovel."

And there they are sitting to this very day.

The Brave Little Tailor

ONE SUMMER morning a little tailor was sitting on his board near the window, and working cheerfully with all his might, when an old woman came down the street crying,

"Good jelly to sell! good jelly to sell!"

The cry sounded pleasant in the little tailor's ears, so he put his head out of the window, and called out,

"Here, my good woman—come here, if you want a customer."

So the poor woman climbed the steps with her heavy basket, and was obliged to unpack and display all her pots to the tailor. He looked at every one of them, and lifting all the lids, applied his nose to each, and said at last,

"The jelly seems pretty good; you may weigh me out four half ounces, or I don't mind having a quarter of a pound."

The woman, who had expected to find a good customer, gave him what he asked for, but went off angry and grumbling.

"This jelly is the very thing for me," cried the

little tailor; "it will give me strength and cunning"; and he took down the bread from the cupboard, cut a whole round of the loaf, and spread the jelly on it, laid it near him, and went on stitching more gallantly than ever. All the while the scent of the sweet jelly was spreading throughout the room, where there were quantities of flies, who were attracted by it and flew to partake.

"Now then, who asked you to come?" said the tailor, and drove the unbidden guests away. But the flies, not understanding his language, were not to be got rid of like that, and returned in larger numbers than before. Then the tailor, not being able to stand it any longer, took from his chimney corner a ragged cloth, and saying,

"Now, I'll let you have it!" beat it among them unmercifully. When he ceased, and counted the slain, he found seven lying dead before him.

"This is indeed somewhat," he said, wondering at his own gallantry; "the whole town shall know this."

So he hastened to cut out a belt, and he stitched it, and put on it in large capitals "Seven at one blow!"

"—The town, did I say!" said the little tailor; "the whole world shall know it!" And his heart quivered with joy, like a lamb's tail.

The tailor fastened the belt round him, and began to think of going out into the world, for his workshop seemed too small for his worship. So he looked about in all the house for something that it would be useful to take with him, but he found nothing but an old cheese, which he put in his pocket. Outside the door he noticed that a bird had got caught in the bushes, so he took that and put it in his pocket with the cheese. Then he set out gallantly on his way, and as he was light and active he felt no fatigue. The way led over a mountain, and when he reached the topmost peak he saw a terrible giant sitting there, and looking about him at his ease. The tailor went bravely up to him, called out to him, and said,

"Comrade, good day! there you sit looking over the wide world! I am on the way thither to seek my fortune: have you a fancy to go with me?"

The giant looked at the tailor contemptuously, and said,

"You little rascal! you miserable fellow!"

"That may be!" answered the little tailor, and undoing his coat he showed the giant his belt; "you can read there whether I am a man or not!"

The giant read: "Seven at one blow!" and thinking it meant men that the tailor had killed, felt at once more respect for the little fellow. But as he wanted to prove him, he took up a stone and squeezed it so hard that water came out of it.

"Now you can do that," said the giant,—"that is, if you have the strength for it."

"That's not much," said the little tailor, "I call that play," and he put his hand in his pocket and

When he reached the topmost peak he saw a terrible giant sitting there, and looking about him at his ease.

took out the cheese and squeezed it, so that the whey ran out of it.

"Well," said he, "what do you think of that?"

The giant did not know what to say to it, for he could not have believed it of the little man. Then the giant took up a stone and threw it so high that it was nearly out of sight.

"Now, little fellow, suppose you do that!"

"Well thrown," said the tailor; "but the stone fell back to earth again,—I will throw you one that will never come back." So he felt in his pocket, took out the bird, and threw it into the air. And the bird, when it found itself at liberty, took wing, flew off, and returned no more.

"What do you think of that, comrade?" asked the tailor.

"There is no doubt that you can throw," said the giant; "but we will see if you can carry."

He led the little tailor to a mighty oak tree which had been felled, and was lying on the ground, and said,

"Now, if you are strong enough, help me to carry this tree out of the wood."

"Willingly," answered the little man; "you take the trunk on your shoulders, I will take the branches with all their foliage, that is much the most difficult."

So the giant took the trunk on his shoulders, and the tailor seated himself on a branch, and the giant, who could not see what he was doing, had the whole tree to carry, and the little man on

it as well. And the little man was very cheerful
and merry, and whistled the tune: *"There were
three tailors riding by,"* as if carrying the tree was
mere child's play. The giant, when he had strug-
gled on under his heavy load a part of the way,
was tired out, and cried,

"Look here, I must let go the tree!"

The tailor jumped off quickly, and taking hold
of the tree with both arms, as if he were carrying
it, said to the giant,

"You see you can't carry the tree though you
are such a big fellow!"

They went on together a little farther, and
presently they came to a cherry tree, and the
giant took hold of the topmost branches, where
the ripest fruit hung, and pulling them down-
wards, gave them to the tailor to hold, bidding
him eat. But the little tailor was much too weak
to hold the tree, and as the giant let go, the tree
sprang back, and the tailor was caught up into
the air. And when he dropped down again without any damage, the giant said to him,

"How is this? haven't you strength enough to
hold such a weak sprig as that?"

"It is not strength that is lacking," answered
the little tailor; "how should it to one who has
slain seven at one blow! I just jumped over the
tree because the hunters are shooting down
there in the bushes. You jump it too, if you can."

The giant made the attempt, and not being
able to vault the tree, he remained hanging in the

branches, so that once more the little tailor got the better of him. Then said the giant,

"As you are such a gallant fellow, suppose you come with me to our den, and stay the night."

The tailor was quite willing, and he followed him. When they reached the den there sat some other giants by the fire, and each had a roasted sheep in his hand, and was eating it. The little tailor looked round and thought,

"There is more elbow-room here than in my workshop."

And the giant showed him a bed, and told him he had better lie down upon it and go to sleep. The bed was, however, too big for the tailor, so he did not stay in it, but crept into a corner to sleep. As soon as it was midnight the giant got up, took a great staff of iron and beat the bed through with one stroke, and supposed he had made an end of that grasshopper of a tailor. Very early in the morning the giants went into the wood and forgot all about the little tailor, and when they saw him coming after them alive and merry, they were terribly frightened, and, thinking he was going to kill them, they ran away in all haste.

So the little tailor marched on, always following his nose. And after he had gone a great way he entered the courtyard belonging to a King's palace, and there he felt so overpowered with fatigue that he lay down and fell asleep. In the meanwhile came various people, who looked at him very curiously, and read on his belt, "Seven at one blow!"

"Oh!" said they, "why should this great lord come here in time of peace? what a mighty champion he must be."

Then they went and told the King about him, and they thought that if war should break out what a worthy and useful man he would be, and that he ought not to be allowed to depart at any price. The King then summoned his council, and sent one of his courtiers to the little tailor to beg him, so soon as he should wake up, to consent to serve in the King's army. So the messenger stood and waited at the sleeper's side until his limbs began to stretch, and his eyes to open, and then he carried his answer back. And the answer was,

"That was the reason for which I came," said the little tailor, "I am ready to enter the King's service."

So he was received into it very honourably, and a separate dwelling set apart for him.

But the rest of the soldiers were very much set against the little tailor, and they wished him a thousand miles away.

"What shall be done about it?" they said among themselves; "if we pick a quarrel and fight with him then seven of us will fall at each blow. That will be of no good to us."

So they came to a resolution, and went all together to the King to ask for their discharge.

"We never intended," said they, "to serve with a man who kills seven at a blow."

The King felt sorry to lose all his faithful servants because of one man, and he wished that he had never seen him, and would willingly get rid of him if he might. But he did not dare to dismiss the little tailor for fear he should kill all the King's people, and place himself upon the throne. He thought a long while about it, and at last made up his mind what to do. He sent for the little tailor, and told him that as he was so great a warrior he had a proposal to make to him. He told him that in a wood in his dominions dwelt two giants, who did great damage by robbery, murder, and fire, and that no man durst go near them for fear of his life. But that if the tailor should overcome and slay both these giants the King would give him his only daughter in marriage, and half his kingdom as dowry, and that a hundred horsemen should go with him to give him assistance.

"That would be something for a man like me!" thought the little tailor, "a beautiful princess and half a kingdom are not to be had every day," and he said to the King,

"Oh yes, I can soon overcome the giants, and yet have no need of the hundred horsemen; he who can kill seven at one blow has no need to be afraid of two."

So the little tailor set out, and the hundred horsemen followed him. When he came to the border of the wood he said to his escort,

"Stay here while I go to attack the giants."

Then he sprang into the wood, and looked about him right and left. After a while he caught sight of the two giants; they were lying down under a tree asleep, and snoring so that all the branches shook. The little tailor, all alive, filled both his pockets with stones and climbed up into the tree, and made his way to an overhanging bough, so that he could seat himself just above the sleepers; and from there he let one stone after another fall on the chest of one of the giants. For a long time the giant was quite unaware of this, but at last he waked up and pushed his comrade, and said,

"What are you hitting me for?"

"You are dreaming," said the other, "I am not touching you." And they composed themselves again to sleep, and the tailor let fall a stone on the other giant.

"What can that be?" cried he, "what are you casting at me?"

"I am casting nothing at you," answered the first, grumbling.

They disputed about it for a while, but as they were tired, they gave it up at last, and their eyes closed once more. Then the little tailor began his game anew, picked out a heavier stone and threw it down with force upon the first giant's chest.

"This is too much!" cried he, and sprang up like a madman and struck his companion such a blow that the tree shook above them. The other paid him back with ready coin, and they fought with such fury that they tore up trees by their roots to use for weapons against each other, so that at last they both of them lay dead upon the ground. And now the little tailor got down.

"Another piece of luck!" said he,—"that the tree I was sitting in did not get torn up too, or else I should have had to jump like a squirrel from one tree to another."

Then he went back to the horsemen and said,

"The deed is done, I have made an end of both of them: but it went hard with me, in the struggle they rooted up trees to defend themselves, but it was of no use, they had to do with a man who can kill seven at one blow."

"Then are you not wounded?" asked the horsemen.

"Nothing of the sort!" answered the tailor, "I have not turned a hair."

The horsemen still would not believe it, and rode into the wood to see, and there they found the giants and all about them lying the uprooted trees.

The little tailor then claimed the promised boon, but the King repented him of his offer, and he sought again how to rid himself of the hero.

"Before you can possess my daughter and the half of my kingdom," said he to the tailor, "you must perform another heroic act. In the wood lives a unicorn who does great damage; you must secure him."

"A unicorn does not strike more terror into me than two giants. Seven at one blow!—that is my way," was the tailor's answer.

So, taking a rope and an axe with him, he went out into the wood, and told those who were ordered to attend him to wait outside. He had not far to seek, the unicorn soon came out and sprang at him, as if he would make an end of him without delay. "Softly, softly," said he, "most haste, worst speed," and remained standing until the animal came quite near, then he slipped quietly behind a tree. The unicorn ran with all his might against the tree and stuck his horn so deep into the trunk that he could not get it out again, and so was taken.

"Now I have you," said the tailor, coming out from behind the tree, and, putting the rope round the unicorn's neck, he took the axe, set free the horn, and when all his party were assembled he led forth the animal and brought it to the King.

The King did not yet wish to give him the promised reward, and set him a third task to do. Before the wedding could take place the tailor was to secure a wild boar which had done a great deal of damage in the wood.

The huntsmen were to accompany him.

"All right," said the tailor, "this is child's play."

But he did not take the huntsmen into the wood, and they were all the better pleased, for the wild boar had many a time before received them in such a way that they had no fancy to disturb him. When the boar caught sight of the tailor he ran at him with foaming mouth and gleaming tusks to bear him to the ground, but the nimble hero rushed into a chapel which chanced to be near, and jumped quickly out of a window on the other side. The boar ran after him, and when he got inside the door shut after him, and there he was imprisoned, for the creature was too big and unwieldy to jump out of the window too. Then the little tailor called the huntsmen that they might see the prisoner with their own eyes; and then he betook himself to the king, who now, whether he liked it or not, was obliged to fulfil his promise, and give him his daughter and the half of his kingdom. But if he had known that the great warrior was only a little tailor he would have taken it still more to heart. So the wedding was celebrated with great splendour and little joy, and the tailor was made into a king.

One night the young queen heard her husband talking in his sleep and saying,

"Now boy, make me that waistcoat and patch me those breeches, or I will lay my yard measure about your shoulders!"

And so, as she perceived of what low birth her husband was, she went to her father the next morning and told him all, and begged him to set her free from a man who was nothing better than a tailor. The king bade her be comforted, saying,

"Tonight leave your bedroom door open, my

guard shall stand outside, and when he is asleep they shall come in and bind him and carry him off to a ship, and he shall be sent to the other side of the world."

So the wife felt consoled, but the king's water-bearer, who had been listening all the while, went to the little tailor and disclosed to him the whole plan.

"I shall put a stop to all this," said he.

At night he lay down as usual in bed, and when his wife thought that he was asleep, she got up, opened the door and lay down again. The little tailor, who only made believe to be asleep, began to murmur plainly,

"Now, boy, make me that waistcoat and patch me those breeches, or I will lay my yard measure about your shoulders! I have slain seven at one blow, killed two giants, caught a unicorn, and taken a wild boar, and shall I be afraid of those who are standing outside my room door?"

And when they heard the tailor say this, a great fear seized them; they fled away as if they had been wild hares, and none of them would venture to attack him.

And so the little tailor all his lifetime remained a king.

Doctor Know-all

ONCE UPON a time a poor Peasant, named Crabb, was taking a load of wood drawn by two oxen to the town for sale. He sold it to a Doctor for four coins. When the money was being paid to him, it so happened that the Doctor was sitting at dinner. When the Peasant saw how daintily the Doctor was eating and drinking, he felt a great desire to become a Doctor too. He remained standing and looking on for a time, and then asked if he could not be a Doctor.

"Oh yes!" said the Doctor; "that is easily managed."

"What must I do?" asked the Peasant.

"First buy an ABC book; you can get one with a cock as a frontispiece. Secondly, turn your wagon and oxen into money, and buy with it clothes and other things suitable for a Doctor. Thirdly, have a sign painted with the words, 'I am Doctor Know-all,' and have it nailed over your door."

The Peasant did everything that he was told to do.

Now when he had been doctoring for a while, not very long though, a rich nobleman had some money stolen from him. He was told about Doctor Know-all, who lived in such and such a village, who would be sure to know what had become of it. So the gentleman ordered his carriage and drove to the village.

He stopped at the Doctor's house, and asked Crabb if he were Doctor Know-all.

"Yes, I am."

"Then you must go with me to get my stolen money back."

"Yes, certainly; but Grethe, my wife, must come too."

The nobleman agreed, and gave both of them seats in his carriage, and they all drove off together.

When they reached the nobleman's castle the dinner was ready, and Crabb was invited to sit down to table.

"Yes; but Grethe, my wife, must dine too"; and he seated himself with her.

When the first Servant brought in a dish of choice food, the Peasant nudged his wife, and said: "Grethe, that was the first,"—meaning that the servant was handing the first dish. But the servant thought he meant, "That was the first thief." As he really was the thief, he became much alarmed, and said to his comrades outside—

"That Doctor knows everything, we shan't

get out of this hole; he said I was the first."

The second Servant did not want to go in at all, but he had to go, and when he offered his dish to the Peasant he nudged his wife, and said—"Grethe, that is the second."

This Servant also was frightened and hurried out.

The third one fared no better. The Peasant said again: "Grethe, that is the third."

The fourth one brought in a covered dish, and the master told the Doctor that he must show his powers and guess what was under the cover. Now it was a dish of crabs.

The Peasant looked at the dish and did not know what to do, so he said: 'Wretched Crabb that I am.'

When the Master heard him he cried: "There, he knows it! Then he knows where the money is too."

Then the Servant grew terribly frightened, and signed to the Doctor to come outside.

When he went out, they all four confessed to him that they had stolen the money; they would gladly give it to him and a large sum in addition, if only he would not betray them to their Master, or their necks would be in peril. They also showed him where the money was hidden. Then the Doctor was satisfied, went back to the table, and said—

"Now, Sir, I will look in my book to see where the money is hidden."

The fifth, in the meantime, had crept into the stove to hear if the Doctor knew still more. But he sat there turning over the pages of his ABC book looking for the cock, and as he could not find it at once, he said: "I know you are there, and out you must come."

The man in the stove thought it was meant for him, and sprang out in a fright, crying: "The man knows everything."

Then Doctor Know-all showed the nobleman where the money was hidden, but he did not betray the servants; and he received much money from both sides as a reward, and became a very celebrated man.

The Seven Ravens

THERE WAS once a Man who had seven sons, but never a daughter, however much he wished for one.

At last, however, he had a daughter.

His joy was great, but the child was small and delicate, and, on account of its weakness, it was to be christened at home.

The Father sent one of his sons in haste to the spring to fetch some water; the other six ran with him, and because each of them wanted to be the first to draw the water, between them the pitcher fell into the brook.

There they stood and didn't know what to do, and not one of them ventured to go home.

As they did not come back, their Father became impatient, and said: "Perhaps the young rascals are playing about, and have forgotten it altogether."

He became anxious lest his little girl should die unbaptized, and in hot vexation, he cried: "I wish the youngsters would all turn into Ravens!"

Scarcely were the words uttered, when he

heard a whirring in the air above his head, and, looking upwards, he saw seven coal-black Ravens flying away.

The parents could not undo the spell, and were very sad about the loss of their seven sons, but they consoled themselves in some measure with their dear little daughter, who soon became strong, and every day more beautiful.

For a long time she was unaware that she had had any brothers, for her parents took care not to mention it.

However, one day by chance she heard some people saying about her: "Oh yes, the girl's pretty enough; but you know she is really to blame for the misfortune to her seven brothers."

Then she became very sad, and went to her father and mother and asked if she had ever had any brothers, and what had become of them.

The parents could no longer conceal the secret. They said, however, that what had happened was by the decree of heaven, and that her birth was merely the innocent occasion.

But the little girl could not get the matter off her conscience for a single day, and thought that she was bound to release her brothers again. She had no peace or quiet until she had secretly set out, and gone forth into the wide world to trace her brothers, wherever they might be, and to free them, let it cost what it might.

She took nothing with her but a little ring as a remembrance of her parents, a loaf of bread against hunger, a pitcher of water against thirst, and a little chair in case of fatigue. She kept ever going on and on until she came to the end of the world.

Then she came to the Sun, but it was hot and terrible; it devoured little children. She ran hastily away to the Moon, but it was too cold, and, moreover, dismal and dreary. And when the child was looking at it, it said: "I smell, I smell man's flesh!"

Then she quickly made off, and came to the Stars, and they were kind and good, and every one sat on his own special seat.

But the Morning Star stood up, and gave her a little bone, and said: "Unless you have this bone, you cannot open the glass mountain, and in the glass mountain are your brothers."

The girl took the bone, and wrapped it up carefully in a little kerchief, and went on again until she came to the glass mountain.

The gate was closed, and she meant to get out the little bone. She undid the kerchief and took out the key to open the glass mountain. Then she fitted it into the keyhole, and succeeded in opening the lock.

When she had entered, she met a Dwarf, who said: "My child, what are you looking for?"

"I am looking for my brothers, the Seven Ravens," she answered.

The Dwarf said: "My masters, the Ravens, are not at home; but if you like to wait until they come, please to walk in."

Thereupon the Dwarf brought in the Ravens' supper, on seven little plates, and in seven little cups, and the little sister ate a crumb or two from each of the little plates, and took a sip from each of the little cups, but she let the ring she had brought with her fall into the last little cup.

All at once a whirring and crying were heard in the air; then the Dwarf said: "Now my masters the Ravens are coming home."

Then they came in, and wanted to eat and drink, and began to look about for their little plates and cups.

But they said one after another: "Halloa! who has been eating off my plate? Who has been drinking out of my cup? There has been some human mouth here."

And when the seventh drank to the bottom of his cup, the ring rolled up against his lips.

He looked at it, and recognised it as a ring belonging to his father and mother, and said: "God grant that our sister may be here, and that we may be delivered."

As the maiden was standing behind the door listening, she heard the wish and came forward, and then all the Ravens got back their human form again.

And they embraced and kissed one another, and went joyfully home.

The Elves and the Shoemaker

THERE WAS once a shoemaker, who, through no fault of his own, became so poor that at last he had nothing left but just enough leather to make one pair of shoes. He cut out the shoes at night, so as to set to work upon them next morning; and as he had a good conscience, he laid himself quietly down in his bed, committed himself to heaven, and fell asleep. In the morning, after he had said his prayers, and was going to get to work, he found the pair of shoes made and finished, and standing on his table. He was very much astonished, and could not tell what to think, and he took the shoes in his hand to examine them more nearly; and they were so well made that every stitch was in its right place, just as if they had come from the hand of a master-workman.

Soon after a purchaser entered, and as the shoes fitted him very well, he gave more than the usual price for them, so that the shoemaker had enough money to buy leather for two more pairs of shoes. He cut them out at night, and intended to set to work the next morning with fresh spirit; but that was not to be, for when he got up they were already finished, and a customer even was not lacking, who gave him so much money that he was able to buy leather enough for four new pairs. Early next morning he found the four pairs also finished, and so it always happened; whatever he cut out in the evening was worked up by the morning, so that he was soon in the way of making a good living, and in the end became very well to do.

One night, not long before Christmas, when the shoemaker had finished cutting out, and before he went to bed, he said to his wife,

"How would it be if we were to sit up tonight and see who it is that does us this service?"

His wife agreed, and set a light to burn. Then they both hid in a corner of the room, behind some coats that were hanging up, and then they began to watch. As soon as it was midnight they saw come in two neatly-formed naked little men, who seated themselves at the shoemaker's table, and took up the work that was already prepared, and began to stitch, to pierce, and to hammer so cleverly and quickly with their little fingers that the shoemaker's eyes could scarcely follow them, so full of wonder was he. And they never left off until everything was finished and was standing ready on the table, and then they jumped up and ran off.

The next morning the shoemaker's wife said to

They took up the work that was already prepared, and began to stitch, to pierce, and to hammer so cleverly and quickly with their little fingers that the shoemaker's eyes could scarcely follow them.

her husband, "Those little men have made us rich, and we ought to show ourselves grateful. With all their running about, and having nothing to cover them, they must be very cold. I'll tell you what; I will make little shirts, coats, waistcoats, and breeches for them, and knit each of them a pair of stockings, and you shall make each of them a pair of shoes."

The husband consented willingly, and at night, when everything was finished, they laid the gifts together on the table, instead of the cut-out work, and placed themselves so that they could observe how the little men would behave. When midnight came, they rushed in, ready to set to work, but when they found, instead of the pieces of prepared leather, the neat little garments put ready for them, they stood a moment in surprise, and then they testified the greatest delight. With the greatest swiftness they took up the pretty garments and slipped them on, singing,

> "What spruce and dandy boys are we!
> No longer cobblers we will be."

Then they hopped and danced about, jumping over the chairs and tables, and at last they danced out at the door.

From that time they were never seen again; but it always went well with the shoemaker as long as he lived, and whatever he took in hand prospered.

The Lady and the Lion

THERE WAS once a Man who had to take a long journey, and when he was saying good-bye to his daughters he asked what he should bring back to them.

The eldest wanted pearls, the second diamonds, but the third said, "Dear father, I should like a singing, soaring lark."

The father said, "Very well, if I can manage it, you shall have it"; and he kissed all three and set off. He bought pearls and diamonds for the two eldest, but he had searched everywhere in vain for the singing, soaring lark, and this worried him, for his youngest daughter was his favourite child.

Once his way led through a wood, in the midst of which was a splendid castle; near it stood a tree, and right up at the top he saw a lark singing and soaring. "Ah," he said, "I have come across you in the nick of time"; and he called to his Servant to dismount and catch the little creature. But as he approached the tree a Lion sprang out from underneath, and shook himself, and roared so that the leaves on the tree trembled.

"Who dares to steal my lark?" said he. "I will eat up the thief!"

Then the Man said, "I didn't know that the bird was yours. I will make up for my fault by paying a heavy ransom. Only spare my life."

But the Lion said, "Nothing can save you, unless you promise to give me whatever first meets you when you get home. If you consent, I will give you your life and the bird into the bargain."

But the Man hesitated, and said, "Suppose my youngest and favourite daughter were to come running to meet me when I go home!"

But the Servant was afraid, and said, "Your daughter will not necessarily be the first to come to meet you; it might just as well be a cat or a dog."

So the Man let himself be persuaded, took the lark, and promised to the Lion for his own whatever first met him on his return home. When he reached home, and entered his house, the first person who met him was none other than his youngest daughter; she came running up and kissed and caressed him, and when she saw that he had brought the singing, soaring lark, she was beside herself with joy. But her father could not rejoice; he began to cry, and said, "My dear child, it has cost me dear, for I have had to promise you to a Lion who will tear you in pieces when he has you in his power." And he told her all that had happened, and begged her not to go, come what might.

But she consoled him, saying, "Dear father, what you have promised must be performed. I will go and will soon soften the Lion's heart, so that I shall come back safe and sound." The next morning the way was shown to her, and she said good-bye and went confidently into the forest.

Now the Lion was an enchanted Prince, who was a Lion by day, and all his followers were Lions too; but by night they reassumed their human form. On her arrival she was kindly received, and conducted to the castle. When night fell, the Lion turned into a handsome man, and their wedding was celebrated with due magnificence. And they lived happily together, sitting up at night and sleeping by day. One day he came to her and said, "Tomorrow there is a festival at your father's house to celebrate your eldest sister's wedding; if you would like to go my Lions shall escort you."

She answered that she was very eager to see her father again, so she went away accompanied by the Lions.

There was great rejoicing on her coming, for they all thought that she had been torn to pieces and had long been dead.

But she told them what a handsome husband she had and how well she fared; and she stayed with them as long as the wedding festivities lasted. Then she went back again into the wood.

When the second daughter married, and the youngest was again invited to the wedding, she said to the Lion, "This time I will not go alone, you must come too."

But the Lion said it would be too dangerous, for if a gleam of light touched him he would be changed into a Dove and would have to fly about for seven years.

"Ah," said she, "only go with me, and I will protect you and keep off every ray of light."

So they went away together, and took their little child with them too. They had a hall built with such thick walls that no ray could penetrate, and thither the Lion was to retire when the wedding torches were kindled. But the door was made of fresh wood which split and caused a little crack which no one noticed.

Now the wedding was celebrated with great splendour. But when the procession came back from church with a large number of torches and lights, a ray of light no broader than a hair fell upon the Prince, and the minute this ray touched him he was changed; and when his wife came in and looked for him, she saw nothing but a White Dove sitting there. The Dove said to her, "For seven years I must fly about the world; every seventh step I will let fall a drop of blood and a white feather which will show you the way, and if you will follow the track you can free me."

Thereupon the Dove flew out of the door, and she followed it, and every seventh step it let fall a drop of blood and a little white feather to show her the way. So she wandered about the world, and never rested till the seven years were nearly passed. Then she rejoiced, thinking that she would soon be free of her troubles; but she was still far from release. One day as they were journeying on in the accustomed way, the feather and the drop of blood ceased falling, and when she looked up the Dove had vanished.

"Man cannot help me," she thought. So she climbed up to the Sun and said to it, "You shine upon all the valleys and mountain peaks, have you not seen a White Dove flying by?"

"No," said the Sun, "I have not seen one; but I will give you a little casket. Open it when you are in dire need."

She thanked the Sun, and went on till night, when the Moon shone out. "You shine all night," she said, "over field and forest, have you seen a White Dove flying by?"

"No," answered the Moon, "I have seen none; but here is an egg. Break it when you are in great need."

She thanked the Moon, and went on till the Night Wind blew upon her. "You blow among all the trees and leaves, have not you seen a White Dove?" she asked.

"No," said the Night Wind, "I have not seen one; but I will ask the other three Winds, who may, perhaps, have seen it."

The East Wind and the West Wind came, but they had seen no Dove. Only the South Wind said, "I have seen the White Dove. It has flown away to the Red Sea, where it has again become a Lion, since the seven years are over; and the Lion is ever fighting with a Dragon who is an enchanted Princess."

Then the Night Wind said, "I will advise you. Go to the Red Sea, you will find tall reeds growing on the right bank; count them, and cut down the eleventh, strike the Dragon with it and then the Lion will be able to master it, and both will regain human shape. Next, look round, and you will see the winged Griffin, who dwells by the Red Sea, leap upon its back with your beloved, and it will carry you across the sea. Here is a nut. Drop it when you come to mid-ocean; it will open immediately and a tall nut tree will grow up out of the water, on which the Griffin will settle. Could it not rest, it would not be strong enough to carry you across, and if you forget to drop the nut, it will let you fall into the sea."

Then she journeyed on, and found everything as the Night Wind had said. She counted the reeds by the sea and cut off the eleventh, struck the Dragon with it, and the Lion mastered it; immediately both regained human form. But when the Princess who had been a Dragon was free from enchantment, she took the Prince in her arms, seated herself on the Griffin's back, and carried him off. And the poor wanderer, again forsaken, sat down and cried. At last she took courage and said to herself: "Wherever the winds blow, I will go, and as long as cocks crow, I will search till I find him."

So she went on a long, long way, till she came to the castle where the Prince and Princess were living. There she heard that there was to be a festival to celebrate their wedding. Then she said to herself, "Heaven help me," and she opened the casket which the Sun had given her; inside it was a dress, as brilliant as the Sun itself. She took it out, put it on, and went into the castle, where every one, including the Bride, looked at her with amazement. The dress pleased the Bride so much that she asked if it was to be bought.

"Not with gold or goods," she answered; "but with flesh and blood."

The Bride asked what she meant, and she answered, "Let me speak with the Bridegroom in his chamber tonight."

The Bride refused. However, she wanted the dress so much that at last she consented; but the Chamberlain was ordered to give the Prince a sleeping draught.

At night, when the Prince was asleep, she was taken to his room. She sat down and said: "For seven years I have followed you. I have been to the Sun, and the Moon, and the Four Winds to look for you. I have helped you against the Dragon, and will you now quite forget me?"

But the Prince slept so soundly that he thought it was only the rustling of the wind among the pine trees. When morning came she was taken away, and had to give up the dress; and as it had not helped her she was very sad, and went out into a meadow and cried. As she was sitting there, she remembered the egg which the Moon had given her; she broke it open, and out came a hen and twelve chickens, all of gold, who ran about chirping, and then crept back under their mother's wings. A prettier sight could not be seen. She got up and drove them about the meadow, till the Bride saw them from the window. The chickens pleased her so much that she asked if they were for sale. "Not for gold and goods, but for flesh and blood. Let me speak with the Bridegroom in his chamber once more."

The Bride said "Yes," intending to deceive her as before; but when the Prince went to his room he asked the Chamberlain what all the murmuring and rustling in the night meant. Then the Chamberlain told him how he had been ordered to give him a sleeping draught because a poor girl had been concealed in his room, and that night he was to do the same again. "Pour out the drink, and put it near my bed," said the Prince. At night she was brought in again, and when she began to relate her sad fortunes he recognised the voice of his dear wife, sprang up, and said, "Now I am really free for the first time. All has been as a dream, for the foreign Princess cast a spell over me so that I was forced to forget you; but heaven in a happy hour has taken away my blindness."

Then they both stole out of the castle, for they feared the Princess's father, because he was a sorcerer. They mounted the Griffin, who bore them over the Red Sea, and when they got to mid-ocean, she dropped the nut. On the spot a fine nut tree sprang up, on which the bird rested; then it took them home, where they found their child grown tall and beautiful, and they lived happily till the end.

The Goose Girl

THERE LIVED once an old Queen, whose husband had been dead many years. She had a beautiful daughter who was promised in marriage to a King's son living a great way off. When the time appointed for the wedding drew near, and the old Queen had to send her daughter into the foreign land, she got together many costly things, furniture and cups and jewels and adornments, both of gold and silver, everything proper for the dowry of a royal Princess, for she loved her daughter dearly. She gave her also a waiting gentlewoman to attend her and to give her into the bridegroom's hands; and they were each to have a horse for the journey, and the Princess's horse was named Falada, and he could speak. When the time for parting came, the old Queen took her daughter to her chamber, and with a little knife she cut her own finger so that it bled; and she held beneath it a white napkin, and on it fell three drops of blood; and she gave it to her daughter, bidding her take care of it, for it would be needful to her on the way. Then they took leave of each other; and the Princess put the napkin in her bosom, got on her horse, and set out to go to the bridegroom. After she had ridden an hour, she began to feel very thirsty, and she said to the waiting woman,

"Get down, and fill my cup that you are carrying with water from the brook; I have great desire to drink."

"Get down yourself," said the waiting woman, "and if you are thirsty stoop down and drink; I will not be your slave."

And as her thirst was so great, the Princess had to get down and to stoop and drink of the water of the brook, and could not have her gold cup to serve her. "Oh dear!" said the poor Princess. And the three drops of blood heard her, and said,

"If your mother knew of this, it would break her heart."

But the Princess answered nothing, and quietly mounted her horse again. So they rode on some miles farther; the day was warm, the sun shone hot, and the Princess grew thirsty once more. And when they came to a water-course she called again to the waiting woman and said,

"Get down, and give me to drink out of my golden cup." For she had forgotten all that had gone before. But the waiting woman spoke still more scornfully and said,

"If you want a drink, you may get it yourself; I am not going to be your slave."

So, as her thirst was so great, the Princess had to get off her horse and to stoop towards the running water to drink, and as she stooped, she wept and said, "Oh dear!" And the three drops of blood heard her and answered,

"If your mother knew of this, it would break her heart!"

And as she drank and stooped over, the napkin on which were the three drops of blood fell out of her bosom and floated down the stream, and in her distress she never noticed it; not so the waiting woman, who rejoiced because she should have power over the bride, who, now that she had lost the three drops of blood, had become weak, and unable to defend herself. And when she was going to mount her horse again the waiting woman cried,

"Falada belongs to me, and this jade to you." And the Princess had to give way and let it be as she said. Then the waiting woman ordered the Princess with many hard words to take off her rich clothing and to put on her plain garments, and then she made her swear to say nothing of the matter when they came to the royal court; threatening to take her life if she refused. And all the while Falada noticed and remembered.

The waiting woman then mounting Falada, and the Princess the sorry jade, they journeyed on till they reached the royal castle. There was great joy at their coming, and the King's son hastened to meet them, and lifted the waiting woman from her horse, thinking she was his bride; and then he led her up the stairs, while the real Princess had to remain below. But the old King, who was looking out of the window, saw her standing in the yard, and noticed how delicate and gentle and beautiful she was, and then he went down and asked the seeming bride who it was that she had brought with her and that was now standing in the courtyard.

"Oh!" answered the bride, "I only brought her with me for company; give the maid something to do, that she may not be for ever standing idle."

But the old King had no work to give her; until he bethought him of a boy he had who took care of the geese, and that she might help him. And so the real Princess was sent to keep geese with the goose boy, who was called Conrad.

Soon after the false bride said to the Prince,

"Dearest husband, I pray thee do me a pleasure."

"With all my heart," answered he.

"Then" said she, "send for the knacker, that he may carry off the horse I came here upon, and make away with him; he was very troublesome to me on the journey." For she was afraid that the horse might tell how she had behaved to the Princess. And when the order had been given that Falada should die, it came to the Princess's ears, and she came to the knacker's man secretly, and promised him a piece of gold if he would do her a service. There was in the town a great dark gateway through which she had to pass morning and evening with her geese, and she asked the man to take Falada's head and to nail it on the gate, that she might always see it as she passed by. And the man promised, and he took Falada's head and nailed it fast in the dark gateway.

Early next morning as she and Conrad drove their geese through the gate, she said as she went by,

> "O Falada, dost thou hang there?"

And the head answered,

> "Princess, dost thou so meanly fare?
> But if thy mother knew thy pain,
> Her heart would surely break in twain."

But she went on through the town, driving her geese to the field. And when they came into the meadows, she sat down and undid her hair, which was all of gold, and when Conrad saw how it glistened, he wanted to pull out a few hairs for himself. And she said,

> "O wind, blow Conrad's hat away,
> Make him run after as it flies,
> While I with my gold hair will play,
> And twist it up in seemly wise."

Then there came a wind strong enough to

blow Conrad's hat far away over the fields, and he had to run after it; and by the time he came back she had put up her hair with combs and pins, and he could not get at any to pull it out; and he was sulky and would not speak to her; so they looked after the geese until the evening came, and then they went home.

The next morning, as they passed under the dark gateway, the Princess said,

> "O Falada, dost thou hang there?"

And Falada answered,

> "Princess, dost thou so meanly fare?
> But if thy mother knew thy pain,
> Her heart would surely break in twain."

And when they reached the fields she sat down and began to comb out her hair; then Conrad came up and wanted to seize upon some of it, and she cried,

> "O wind, blow Conrad's hat away,
> Make him run after as it flies,
> While I with my gold hair will play,
> And do it up in seemly wise."

Then the wind came and blew Conrad's hat very far away, so that he had to run after it, and when he came back again her hair was put up

Then the wind came and blew Conrad's hat very far away, so that he had to run after it.

again, so that he could pull none of it out; and
they tended the geese until the evening.

And after they had got home, Conrad went to
the old King and said, "I will tend the geese no
longer with that girl!"

"Why not?" asked the old King.

"Because she vexes me the whole day long,"
answered Conrad. Then the old King ordered
him to tell how it was.

"Every morning," said Conrad, "as we pass
under the dark gateway with the geese, there is
an old horse's head hanging on the wall, and she
says to it,

> "O Falada, dost thou hang there?"

And the head answers,

> "Princess, dost thou so meanly fare?
> But if thy mother knew thy pain,
> Her heart would surely break in twain."

And besides this, Conrad related all that happened in the fields, and how he was obliged to
run after his hat.

The old King told him to go to drive the geese
next morning as usual, and he himself went
behind the gate and listened how the maiden
spoke to Falada; and then he followed them into
the fields, and hid himself behind a bush; and he

watched the goose boy and the goose girl tend the geese; and after a while he saw the girl make her hair all loose, and how it gleamed and shone. Soon she said,

> "O wind, blow Conrad's hat away,
>   And make him follow as it flies,
>   While I with my gold hair will play,
>   And bind it up in seemly wise."

Then there came a gust of wind and away went Conrad's hat, and he after it, while the maiden combed and bound up her hair; and the old King saw all that went on. At last he went unnoticed away, and when the goose girl came back in the evening he sent for her, and asked the reason of her doing all this.

"That I dare not tell you," she answered, "nor can I tell any man of my woe, for when I was in danger of my life I swore an oath not to reveal it." And he pressed her sore, and left her no peace, but he could get nothing out of her. At last he said,

"If you will not tell it me, tell it to the iron oven," and went away. Then she crept into the iron oven, and began to weep and to lament, and at last she opened her heart and said,

"Here I sit forsaken of all the world, and I am a King's daughter, and a wicked waiting woman forced me to give up my royal garments and my

place at the bridegroom's side, and I am made a
goose girl, and have to do mean service. And if
my mother knew, it would break her heart."

Now the old King was standing outside by the
oven door listening, and he heard all she said,
and he called to her and told her to come out of
the oven. And he caused royal clothing to be put
upon her, and it was a marvel to see how
beautiful she was. The old King then called his
son and proved to him that he had the wrong
bride, for she was really only a waiting woman,
and that the true bride was here at hand, she
who had been the goose girl. The Prince was
glad at heart when he saw her beauty and gentle-
ness; and a great feast was made ready, and all
the court people and good friends were bidden
to it. The bridegroom sat in the midst with the
Princess on one side and the waiting woman on
the other; and the false bride did not know the
true one, because she was dazzled with her
glittering braveries. When all the company had
eaten and drunk and were merry, the old King
gave the waiting woman a question to answer,
as to what such an one deserved, who had
deceived her masters in such and such a man-
ner, telling the whole story, and ending by
asking,

"Now, what doom does such an one deserve?"

"No better than this," answered the false bride,
"that she be put naked into a cask, studded
inside with sharp nails, and be dragged along in

it by two white horses from street to street, until she be dead."

"Thou hast spoken thy own doom," said the old King; "as thou hast said, so shall it be done." And when the sentence was fulfilled, the Prince married the true bride, and ever after they ruled over their kingdom in peace and blessedness.

Jorinda and Joringel

THERE WAS once an old castle in the middle of a vast thick wood; in it there lived an old woman quite alone, and she was a witch. By day she made herself into a cat or a screech-owl, but regularly at night she became a human being again. In this way she was able to decoy wild beasts and birds, which she would kill, and boil or roast. If any man came within a hundred paces of the castle, he was forced to stand still and could not move from the place till she gave the word of release; but if an innocent maiden came within the circle she changed her into a bird,and shut her up in a cage which she carried into a room in the castle. She must have had seven thousand cages of this kind, containing pretty birds.

Now, there was once a maiden called Jorinda who was more beautiful than all other maidens. She had promised to marry a very handsome youth named Joringel, and it was in the days of their courtship, when they took the greatest joy in being alone together, that one day they wandered out into the forest. "Take care," said Joringel; "do not let us go too near the castle."

It was a lovely evening. The sunshine glanced between the tree trunks of the dark green wood, while the turtledoves sang plaintively in the old beech trees. Yet Jorinda sat down in the sunshine, and could not help weeping and bewailing, while Joringel, too, soon became just as mournful. They both felt as miserable as if they had been going to die. Gazing round them, they found they had lost their way, and did not know how they should find the path home. Half the sun still appeared above the mountain; half had sunk below. Joringel peered into the bushes and saw the old walls of the castle quite close to them; he was terror-struck, and became pale as death. Jorinda was singing:

> "My birdie with its ring so red
>   Sings sorrow, sorrow, sorrow;
> My love will mourn when I am dead,
>   Tomorrow, morrow, mor——jug, jug."

Joringel looked at her, but she was changed into a nightingale who sang "Jug, Jug."

A screech-owl with glowing eyes flew three times round her, and cried three times "Shu hu-hu." Joringel could not stir; he stood like a stone without being able to speak, or cry, or move hand or foot. The sun had now set; the owl flew into a bush, out of which appeared almost at the same moment a crooked old woman, skinny and yellow; she had big, red eyes and a crooked nose whose tip reached her chin. She mumbled something, caught the nightingale, and carried it away in her hand. Joringel could not say a word nor move from the spot, and the nightingale was gone. At last the old woman came back, and said in a droning voice: "Greeting to thee, Zachiel! When the moon shines upon the cage, unloose the captive, Zachiel!"

Then Joringel was free. He fell on his knees before the witch, and implored her to give back his Jorinda; but she said he should never have her again, and went away. He pleaded, he wept, he lamented, but all in vain. "Alas! what is to become of me?" said Joringel. At last he went away, and arrived at a strange village, where he spent a long time as a shepherd. He often wandered round about the castle, but did not go too near it. At last he dreamt one night that he found a blood-red flower, in the midst of which was a beautiful large pearl. He plucked the flower, and took it to the castle. Whatever he touched with it was made free of enchantment. He dreamt, too, that by this means he had found his Jorinda again. In the morning when he awoke he began to search over hill and dale, in the hope of finding a flower like this; he searched till the ninth day, when he found the flower early in the morning. In the middle was a big dewdrop, as big as the finest pearl. This flower he carried day and night, till he reached the castle. He was not held fast as before when he came within the hundred paces of the castle, but walked straight up to the door.

Joringel was filled with joy; he touched the door with the flower, and it flew open. He went in through the court, and listened for the sound of birds. He went on, and found the hall, where the witch was feeding the birds in the seven thousand cages. When she saw Joringel she was angry, very angry—scolded, and spat poison and gall at him. He paid no attention to her, but turned away and searched among the bird-cages. Yes, but there were many hundred nightingales; how was he to find his Jorinda?

While he was looking about in this way he noticed that the old woman was secretly removing a cage with a bird inside, and was making for the door. He sprang swiftly towards her, touched the cage and the witch with the flower, and then she no longer had power to exercise her spells. Jorinda stood there, as beautiful as before, and threw her arms round Joringel's neck. After that he changed all the other birds back into maidens again, and went home with Jorinda, and they lived long and happily together.

The Twelve Dancing Princesses

THERE WAS once a King who had twelve daughters, each more beautiful than the other. They slept together in a hall where their beds stood close to one another; and at night, when they had gone to bed, the King locked the door and bolted it. But when he unlocked it in the morning, he noticed that their shoes had been danced to pieces, and nobody could explain how it happened. So the King sent out a proclamation saying that any one who could discover where the Princesses did their night's dancing should choose one of them to be his wife and should reign after his death; but whoever presented himself, and failed to make the discovery after three days and nights, was to forfeit his life.

A Prince soon presented himself and offered to take the risk. He was well received, and at night was taken into a room adjoining the hall where the Princesses slept. His bed was made up there, and he was to watch and see where they went to dance; so that they could not do anything, or go anywhere else, the door of his

84